ARTHUR

AND THE

WITCH

Johanne Mercier

Daniel Hahn

Clare Elsom

More stories with Arthur

CONTENTS

For Mado, who makes the best
blueberry pies

JM

For Lucas

DH

For Graeme

CE

Chapter 1
The Blueberries

I'm Arthur and I'm seven, and last Saturday, at my grandparents' house at Picket Lake, I discovered a secret hiding place; a hiding place filled with blueberries. I picked hundreds of them as a surprise for Grandma. I ate a few of them, too.

When I arrived back home with a full basket, she was really impressed.

Grandma took out a rolling pin, some flour and everything you need to make a pie.

Grandad and I sat down at the table, each of us with a fork and a small plate.

And we waited.

The whole house was filled with the smell of blueberries.

We needed to be patient.

That pie took its time cooking.

Then Grandma pulled on her big oven gloves.

"Oh, how wonderful, Margaret!" said Grandad, when she opened the oven door. "Where did you find the blueberries, Arthur?"

"At the end of the lake," I replied.

Grandma nearly dropped the pie on the floor.

"At the end… the end… of the lake?" she repeated in a trembling voice.

"Yes."

She had gone pale. She looked nervously at Grandad. Then she leaned towards me and asked quietly: "Arthur, dear, did you really wander down as far as the end of the lake?"

"Yes."

"On the land where you found the blueberries, did you see an old grey house?"

"Yes."

"With dirty window panes, a rusty roof and cobwebs?"

"I'm not sure about the cobwebs."

Grandma put her hand on her heart, like she always does when she's really nervous. Then she whispered something in Grandad's ear, so I wouldn't be able to hear.

"He took the blueberries from the witch."

But I heard perfectly well.

As for Grandad, he didn't look worried at all.

"Geoffrey, do you remember what happened to Joe Barnet when he ate the witch's blueberries?" my grandmother whispered.

Grandad didn't have time to reply. Grandma had already picked up the telephone, saying: "I must ask Eugene! I'm sure he'll be able to help!"

"What happened to Joe Barnet?" I asked.
But no one answered.

Chapter 2
Danger! Beware!

When Eugene rushed into my grandparents' house, Grandma gave a huge sigh of relief.

"Ah, Eugene dear! Thank goodness we can count on you!"

Eugene didn't even say "hello". He just looked at the pie, stammering, "Is that… Is that it?"

"Yes," murmured Grandma. "The witch's blueberries are all inside."

Cousin Eugene took a few steps back.

Then he announced: "Nobody get too close, understand? After what happened to Joe Barnet, we can't be too careful."

I asked again what had happened to Joe Barnet.

Grandad rolled his eyes.

"It's just a story, Arthur. The house has been empty for..."

"And the hay fever that Joe Barnet hasn't been able to shake off since he ate the

witch's blueberries. You really think that's just a story, Uncle Geoffrey?"

"And his hiccupping attacks during the night?" added Grandma.

"And his hens that only lay eggs once a week?" Eugene went on.

"Oh, the poor man," sighed my grandmother. "Ah, she never forgives you, that witch at the end of the lake. She couldn't be more spiteful where her blueberries are concerned."

I put my hand on my tummy.

"Are the blueberries poisoned?" I asked.

"Nobody knows, young man!" Eugene replied. "Nobody knows."

I didn't dare to tell them that I'd eaten loads and loads of them on my way back from the witch's house.

Chapter 3
The Witch's Revenge

Eugene announced that he would stay with us all day, but everything was fine: I didn't have a tummy ache; I didn't get hiccups; or hay fever; or anything. The witch had probably just decided not to take revenge.

Nobody had touched the pie. It was sitting on the table. Eugene had covered it with a cloth while they were waiting to make a decision. He suggested that he could take it back to his place and burn it.

Grandad was against the idea. Grandma wanted a bit of time to think. Eugene said it was important to do something before it was too late.

I realised he was right towards the end of the afternoon... when things started to go wrong.

First of all, there was the gravy, which Grandma had to start again four times.

"I've never got gravy wrong before," she grumbled at each attempt, as she poured a lumpy kind of liquid down the sink. "This is not normal."

Then there was the bag from the vacuum cleaner, which exploded in the living room while Eugene was trying to help with the housework.

"This is unusual, too; an exploding vacuum cleaner," Eugene kept repeating, as he cleaned up the mess.

And later, when I wanted to turn on the television… BANG! All the fuses blew. There was no electricity anywhere in the house.

"It's most irregular, this blackout, Aunt Margaret! Most irregular."

It was at that moment that we heard a noise; a terrible BOOM, as if the sky were falling on our heads. I threw myself into Grandma's arms. Eugene rushed to hide under the table.

"It's the wi… it's the witch!" cried Eugene.

"No, it's not. It's thunder," said Grandad calmly.

"I can assure you, it's the terrible witch at the end of the lake, taking her revenge, Uncle Geoffrey! First the gravy, then

the vacuum cleaner, then the fuses, the blackout… and now a hurricane!"

"We have to do something!" said Grandma.

I was starting to feel a bit scared.

Chapter 4
The Letter

Grandad went outside. Through the living-room window I could see the wind blowing so strongly that branches were coming off the big maple tree behind the house. I'd never seen clouds that black before.

Out in the garden, Grandad was collecting up the bits of shingle that were falling off the roof, and running after all the things that were being blown around by the wind.

As for Grandma, she rushed over to the cabinet in the living room. She opened the drawer and took out a sheet of paper, a pencil and an envelope.

"We're going to write to the witch to say sorry," she announced.

"That is undoubtedly the right thing to do!" said Eugene.

He crept out from under the table and got up, grimacing. Then he took the pencil and Grandma dictated the first few words.

"Dear Witch at the End of the Lake…"

"Won't she get angry?" I asked. "Maybe she doesn't like people calling her a witch."

"Arthur's right. Start again, Eugene.
Dear Lady from the End of the Lake…"

"I'd say *Dear Madam from the End of the Lake* instead," Eugene suggested.

"*Very Dear Madam from the End of the Lake?*" added Grandma.

"*Very Dear Madam who we like Very, Very Much?*"

"Surely not!"

They argued like this over every sentence.

"This is quite normal, Arthur,"

Grandma explained to me. "When you're addressing a witch, you need to choose your words carefully."

When Grandad got back, he read the letter.

"Very Dear Madam from the End of the Lake,

We would like to apologise for the blueberries. We can understand why you are angry: the gravy, the fuses, the vacuum cleaner, the storm and everything.

So, Cousin Eugene is bringing you the pie. All your blueberries are inside.

Enjoy!

Yours,

The Franklin Family.

"NOT OUR PIE!" cried Grandad.

"We have to do what we have to do, Geoffrey," Grandma replied firmly. "We cannot remain under the same roof as this pie."

"It is unquestionably a threat to us," added Eugene.

"There is no way we're giving our dessert to that nasty witch!"

"But you said she didn't exist, Grandad!"

"Exactly, Arthur! Not only does this witch not exist, but she does not deserve any pie!"

Eugene was already getting ready to leave.

His mind was made up.

"I'd like to take some garlic," he said.

Grandma wrinkled up her nose.

"Garlic? Why garlic? Better to take her some cream, instead. That will go much better with the pie."

"Garlic drives away witches, Aunt Margaret. I might need some if she's angry."

Grandad sighed.

"Garlic is for driving away vampires, Eugene, not witches! You're getting everything muddled up."

"Do you believe in vampires, Grandad?"

"Er… no, Arthur."

"Do you believe in witches?"

"Not in the least."

"All I've got are these onions," announced Grandma, rummaging through the larder. "Do you want to take some onions, Eugene?"

"And some spuds and turnips, too?"
Grandad grumbled.

Brave Eugene announced that he was
ready. He was going to face the danger
for us.

"Be very careful, Eugene," said
Grandma, handing him the pie.

"Mmm…" said Eugene, sniffing the scent of blueberries, his eyes closed.

"Concentrate, Eugene!" snapped Grandma. "You're to put it outside her door and run straight back. Understand?"

We sat on the porch and watched Eugene making his way into the forest with the blueberry pie, the little note for the witch and the onions.

There wasn't a single cloud in the sky.

"What a waste of a lovely pie," grumbled Grandad.

Chapter 5
Which Witch?

Eugene didn't hang around the witch's house for long. All the same, when he came back he was completely exhausted, his clothes were dirty, and his hair all messed up.

"I have some amazing news for you!" he said, still breathless.

"Did the witch run after you?" I asked. "Did she cast an evil spell on you? Did she try and put you in her cauldron? Turn you into a frog?"

"No, no, no and no. You'd better sit down on the sofa. This news might just astonish you."

Grandma and I did as we were told. Eventually, Grandad came over to sit down, too.

"Well, my dear friends, I have the honour of informing you that the house at the end of the lake doesn't have a witch living in it at all!"

Grandad gave me a wink. "You see, Arthur? I was right."

"Are you completely sure, Eugene?" asked Grandma.

"Completely."

Grandma looked relieved. And I must confess, I was relieved, too. It's always good to discover that the blueberries you've eaten haven't been poisoned by a witch.

But Eugene added in a slightly spooky voice, "There isn't a witch living in it, anymore, but..."

Grandma squeezed my hand.

"I saw her ghooooost!"

"You saw a real, flesh-and-blood ghost, Eugene?" asked Grandma.

"I did!"

"The ghost of the witch?"

"The ghost of which witch?" growled Grandad. "As I've told you..."

"Oh, I am quite certain, Uncle Geoffrey."

"Anyhow, the good news is that ghosts never eat dessert!" announced Grandad, heading for the kitchen.

He took out the little plates and the forks, tied a napkin around his neck and asked, "So, where is the pie, Eugene?"

Eugene blushed, but didn't answer.

"Don't tell me you forgot it!"

"No, not at all."

"Did you lose it?"

"Absolutely not."

"Did you leave it for the ghost?"

I was the one who asked that question.

"Where have you put my pie?" insisted Grandad.

"It's been… How should I put it? Devoured!" Eugene mumbled.

"Devoured?" repeated Grandma.

"Precisely! Devoured by the ghost at the end of the lake!"

He looked up and gave a big smile.

And this time, we all stared at Eugene wide-eyed.

Nobody believed his story about the ghost of the witch at the end of the lake anymore. Not even Grandma.

Because we could all see that Cousin Eugene's teeth were completely blue!

ARTHUR

Johanne Mercier

It all started when this lady called Johanne thought about me in her head. Grandma said Johanne had written fifty-eight stories for children, and that one of her stories was made into a film. Grandma also said Johanne understands children because she used to be a teacher. But now she writes all day.

I think it must be really fun to write stories all day. When I grow up, I want to write stories like Johanne Mercier, and I also want to be a pilot. Grandad says there's nothing to stop me doing both, but I think that writing stories and flying a plane at the same time is not a good idea.

Daniel Hahn

Daniel Hahn translated the stories. He took my French words, and wrote them in English. He said it was quite a difficult job, but Cousin Eugene said he could have done it much better, only he was busy that day. So we got Daniel to do it, as he's translated loads and loads of books before. He also said he wrote the words for a book called *Happiness is a Watermelon on your Head*, but everyone else said that book was just plain silly.

Daniel is almost as clever as Cousin Eugene and he lives in England, in a house by the sea, with a lot of books.

Clare Elsom

I was so happy when we met Clare Elsom. She got out her pencils and pens and scribbled until the scribbles looked just like me! Grandma and Grandad said the resemblance was uncanny.

Clare has so many pencils and pens – at least twenty of them – and she spends all day drawing in lots of different books. I'm not sure that you are allowed to draw in books, but she seems to get away with it.

I like Clare because she likes egg on toast and exploring new places, and drawing me. But I think she wants my pet duck, so I will have to keep an eye on her.

More escapades with
Arthur coming soon

Arthur and the Ice Rink

Also available

ARTHUR

AND THE

ICE RINK

JOHANNE MERCIER

Arthur and the Witch
ISBN: 978-1-907912-20-7

First published in French in 2008 under the title *Arthur et la Sorcière du Bout du Lac*
by Dominique et compagnie, a division of Les Editions Heritage, Saint-Lambert,
Canada. This edition published in the UK by Phoenix Yard Books Ltd, 2013.

Phoenix Yard Books
Phoenix Yard
65 King's Cross Road
London
WC1X 9LW
www.phoenixyardbooks.com

Text copyright © Johanne Mercier, 2008
English translation copyright © Daniel Hahn, 2013
Illustrations copyright © Clare Elsom, 2013

1 3 5 7 9 10 8 6 4 2
A CIP catalogue record for this book is available from the British Library
Printed in China